A Kiss Goodbye

Audrey Penn

Illustrated by

Barbara L. Gibson

Tanglewood • Terre Haute, IN

Published by Tanglewood Press, LLC, April 2007.

Text © Audrey Penn 2007.
Illustrations © Barbara Leonard Gibson 2007.

Design by Amy Alick Perich

Tanglewood Press, LLC
P. O. Box 3009
Terre Haute, IN 47803
www.tanglewoodbooks.com

Printed in China

10 9 8 7 6 5 4 3 2 1

ISBN 978-1-933718-04-0
        1-933718-04-8

Library of Congress Cataloging-in-Publication Data

Penn, Audrey, 1947-
   A kiss goodbye / Audrey Penn ; illustrated by Barbara Leonard Gibson.
      p. cm.
   Summary: Chester Raccoon is very unhappy about leaving his home, a tree that has been marked by tree cutters, but his mother tries to convince him that their new home might be even better.
   ISBN-10: 1-933718-04-8 (hardcover w/jacket)
   ISBN-13: 978-1-933718-03-3
   [1. Moving, Household--Fiction. 2. Family life--Fiction. 3. Raccoons--Fiction.] I. Gibson, Barbara, ill. II. Title.

PZ7.P38448Khs 2007
[E]--dc22
                                            2006037882

To all my friends, big and little, who find
their way to the other end of the path.
-AP

For Robert, Caitlin, and Mom
-BLG

Chester Raccoon sat in the corner of his tree hollow and frowned. "I'm not moving," he announced stubbornly. "I'm staying here. I want to stay with my tree, and stay with my friends, and stay where I've always lived."

Mrs. Raccoon patted Chester's worried, furrowed forehead. "I understand how you feel," she told him in an understanding, motherly voice, "but I'm afraid we all have to move."

"But I like it here," whined Chester. "It's my home."

"It's my home, too," said Mrs. Raccoon. "And Ronny's. And I know how scary it is to move to a new place. But sometimes, like when you started school and changed classes, you have to do things that are scary and hard at first. I know—maybe you could think of moving as an adventure."

Chester scrunched up his face and grumbled.
"I don't like adventures. I had an adventure down
at the pond and fell in chasing a frog."

"I had an adventure up a pine tree
and got prickly pinecones in my tail!"

"I had an adventure in Red Rock Cave
and got smacked by a bat!"

Mrs. Raccoon laughed. "Well, this will be a different kind of adventure. This time we'll all be together. You and me and Ronny."

Chester didn't budge. He just sat there with his arms folded and a stubborn expression on his face. "Why do we have to leave our tree, anyway?" he wanted to know. "I like this tree. I'm used to it."

"A line has been drawn around the trunk," explained Mrs. Raccoon. "Soon the tree cutters will come and cut it down for wood."

Chester poked his head out of the hollow and looked around. "There are lots of other trees," he pointed out. "Why don't they cut down some of the other trees instead?"

"They're cutting down all of the trees in this part of the woods," explained his mother. "But I've picked out a new tree to live in that's big and comfortable and has lots of holes to look out of."

Chester sat back down and looked thoughtful. "What if I don't leave? What if I just sit here and never leave this tree again as long as I live? Will they still cut it down?"

"I'm afraid they would," said Mrs. Raccoon. "But you know, moving isn't so bad. I've moved lots of times. It's hard at first, but you make new friends and fix up your new tree just the way you like it. Besides, don't you think you'll get a little lonely if you stay here? The deer are moving, and the squirrels, and so are the skunks and foxes. Don't you want to stay with your family?"

"Will I have to go to a new school?" asked Chester.

"I suppose you will. But you never know who you might meet. Don't you want to make new friends?"

"I like the friends I already have. I don't need to make new ones."

"I see. Well, I would certainly miss you if you stayed here," said Mrs. Raccoon. "Aren't you afraid you'd miss us?"

"I'd miss you," admitted Chester. "I'm not so sure about Ronny."

Mrs. Raccoon chuckled. "I think you'd miss Ronny most of all. Who would be there to pull your tail or tickle your mask or follow you everywhere you went?"

Chester sat back and took a good, long look around the inside of his hollow. He memorized its round shape with its lookout hole just below the thick branches that housed bird nests and squirrels. Then he closed his eyes, pressed his palms to the wall, and felt the texture of the wood and bark—the smooth places and the rough places. When he opened his eyes, he reached up and broke off a small piece of bark from the wall and pushed it deep into his pocket.

When Chester climbed outside, he wrapped his little arms around the tree trunk and said goodbye again. This time, a tiny tear rolled down his cheek.

Chester stayed quiet all the way to the far end of the distant woods. When he arrived at his new tree in the morning, he folded his arms and pouted.

Mrs. Raccoon nuzzled him on the ear. "Why don't we all go inside and see how we like it."

Chester followed his mother and brother into the tree hollow and looked around. He reached into his pocket and fingered the small piece of bark he had brought with him. It felt good having a piece of his old home.

"What do you think?" asked Mrs. Raccoon.

"It's okay," said Chester.

Ronny looked up at his big brother, saw that he was sad, and climbed onto his lap. Reaching up, he pulled Chester's whiskers and tickled him under his arm. Chester couldn't help but giggle.

"I miss my tree," he told Ronny.

"I do, too," came a sweet voice from outside.

Chester's ears perked up and he
popped his head out of the hollow.
There, standing at the foot of the tree,
was a young raccoon just about his age.
"Hi. I'm Cassy," said the young
raccoon. "Who are you?"

Chester ducked back down into the hollow and brushed back his ruffled black mask. When he popped his head back out, Cassy was still there. "I'm Chester," he said shyly. "Do you live here?"

"I do now," said Cassy.

Chester left Ronny with his mother, climbed out of the tree, and stood beside the pretty raccoon. His tiny pink cheeks plumbed into a wide smile.

Mrs. Raccoon peeked out of the tree and grinned. Placing a kiss in her palm, she showed it to Chester and told him to go play.

Chester kissed the center of his palm and turned it toward his mother. "All right," he told her. "I'll stay."